Dripping
A Poetry Collection

Farzana Habib

Ukiyoto Publishing

All global publishing rights are held by

Ukiyoto Publishing

Published in 2024

Content Copyright © Farzana Habib
ISBN 9789364947817

*All rights reserved.
No part of this publication may be reproduced,
transmitted, or stored in a retrieval system, in any form
by any means, electronic, mechanical, photocopying,
recording or otherwise, without the prior permission of
the publisher.*

The moral rights of the authors have been asserted.

*This is a work of fiction. Names, characters, businesses,
places, events, locales, and incidents are either the
products of the author's imagination or used in a fictitious
manner. Any resemblance to actual persons, living or
dead, or actual events is purely coincidental.*

*This book is sold subject to the condition that it shall not by
way of trade or otherwise, be lent, resold, hired out or
otherwise circulated, without the publisher's prior
consent, in any form of binding or cover other than that in
which it is published.*

www.ukiyoto.com

These poems are dedicated to the broken hearts in the world

Contents

Ring	1
Signs II	2
Loved	3
Disagreement	5
Unaturally Natural	6
Love Language	9
Untitled	11
Space	13
Chest Pains	15
Kill	17
Universal	18
Life	19
A Love Poem	20
Black	21
Waiting	22
Aimless	23
The Sun and The Moon	25
Penalty	26

Playing by the Rules	27
Transitions	29
About the Author	*29*

Ring

The phone rings
Once twice thrice
My heart would beat faster with every ring
Until I heard those magical words on the other end
Hi My Love

The phone still rings
Once twice thrice
My heart sinks a little more with each ring now
Cause I know that you will not come to the phone anymore

Signs II

Missed phone calls
Hourly text messages
Morning plans
Late night texting
Notes and Reminders
New plans and schedules
Regular check-ins
Unlimited hugs and kisses
Emoji galore

Each one a symbol of my love
He called them love bombs

Loved

I loved talking to you
That is why I would talk nonstop

I loved listening to you
That is why I would make excuses to stay on the phone longer

I loved looking at you
That is why I would sit in the front seat

I loved holding you in my arms
That is why I would always watch you fall asleep first

I loved holding hands with you
That is why I would always keep them in mine

I loved texting you

Dripping

That is why I would often rush through the day and find ways to talk to you

I loved kissing you
That is why I could never stop at just one

I loved being touched by you
That is why I gave myself to you

Disagreement

Tis better to have loved and lost
Than never to have loved at all.

I must disagree
It hurts both ways

Unnaturally Natural

Long conversations

Cute pet names

Compliments

Words of affirmation

Support

Comfort

Strength

Peace

An answer to every question

Counting down minutes

Pickups and drop offs

Waiting by the phone

Hand holding

Hugs from the back

Forehead kisses

Cuddles in the car

Long walks

Leg messages

Talking about the future

Marriage and kids

3 kids

2 dogs

Apartment on the 25th floor

I tried extremely hard to not get my feelings in the way of all of that

You said all the right things

You did all the right things

I fell for you

Not at first but harder than most

To the point I could no longer resist

I asked questions the entire way

I took a chance

Followed my heart

Everything seemed perfect

I still could not believe it

I am grateful for the experience

Dripping

For you
A man who had everything I wanted and more
A man whom I thought I deserved

Still never got the ending that I wanted

Love Language

I think I messed up

Too many phone calls

Too many missed calls

Never ending messages

The need to constantly see you

The overwhelming desires

To caress

To embrace

To kiss

To become one

I thought this was the equivalent of I love, and I miss you

I thought this was better than I am sorry and forgive me

I did everything out of love and compassion

I thought about you a little more than I did of myself

It was love over life

Dripping

You meant both to me

You thought it was all ok until it was not ok anymore

I wish you had explained things to me instead of leaving me behind with no answers

Untitled

Time passes by
Minutes turn into hours
Morning into night
Light to dark

Sometimes time stands still for me.
The world is a blur
I somehow feel stuck
There are no daydreams
No nightmares
I think of you often
Memories continue to play over repeatedly like an old movie reel
I begin to loath reality
The very idea of a life without you
It is hard to accept
Even harder to imagine

Dripping

I wish I was small

Small enough to fit inside my own mind

Small enough to walk through the doors of our own little world

Just you and I

Where things are perfect

Never ending

Space

What does it mean when someone asks for space

I gave you enough space to come close to me

I gave you space to think and plan

I gave you space in my head.

I gave you space in my heart

I gave you space in my life

But that's not what you wanted

You wanted space away from me

To think, move and plan

I want to say that I understand

But I do not actually

I do not understand the concept at all

I talk things through

I sleep on it

I read and research

Ask for second opinions even

I always come back to you

Dripping

You need space now
Days on end
I tried to respect your boundaries
I really tried respect your privacy
After some time, I failed to do both
It might be love or weakness on my part
I still don't understand the concept of space

Chest Pains

It starts in my chest and radiates all over the body

It feels like there's a hole in my heart now

It hurts in the morning

It aches in the afternoon.

It burns in the evening

It bleeds at night

It gets bigger with time

It always stays empty

I do not know what to fill it with anymore.

Family, friends, work and play did not work at all

Drugs and alcohol only numb the pain

Sleep and rest only awaken the pain.

My clothes conceal it

But the truth remains the same

I am still in pain

It stabs me in the morning

Dripping

It grabs me in the afternoon
It strangles me in the evening
It kills me at night.

Kill

Not being able to talk to you, it hurts emotionally

Not being able to see you hurt physically

Not being able to be with you by just kills me

Kills all the parts of me that you love

Kills all the parts of me that I hate but you me made me love again

Kills my smile that has reappeared after so many years

Kills my dreams one by one

Kills my peace of mind

Universal

This has been said by many lovers
In past history and modern times
I would kill for you
I would die for you
I would die without you

Sounds painful
Even romantic to some
But quite easy when you really think about it
Love is not about the end
Love is not about leaving

It is more of a journey for the heart, mind and soul
With a beginning, middle and end.

Life

I hope everyone finds a person
Who will live for them
Since death follows us everywhere.

A Love Poem

Love me the same way your poems are written on paper

Let paper be my skin

Let each letter be a kiss

Let one word be a single touch

Let one sentence be a long embrace

Let one stanza be the sounds and feelings of love and desire

Black

Blood shows up on anything with color
Paint my heart black then
So that the pain I feel will not be visible to anyone
Much less to the naked eye

Waiting

Please come back

Before the henna stain leaves my fingers and hands

Before your name fades away

This was supposed to be about the two of us

Not just the memories that float about in this broken heart of mine

Aimless

Still no answer
Still no response
I had lost my mind for a little bit
At first it was all in my head
Then I began to lose other things
Sleep
Focus
Clarity
Strength
I questioned my heart all the time
I prayed till my hands ached
I wrote till my fingers bled
I walked till my feet became sore
The road ahead of me is still not clear
I do not know where to go
How to move ahead

Dripping

I know I do not want to go back to the past either.

The Sun and The Moon

You and I are like the sun and moon
Both unique in their own ways
Full of beauty and wonder
You shine while I glow
Appreciated from a distance
Never meant to be together

Penalty

Do the crime, do the time they say

Falling in love was the crime

What is so criminal about it

I lost myself in you

Completely

Internally and externally

I am not ashamed of the way I loved you

However, I wonder why the penalty of a crime is so great

I will see you today

Maybe tomorrow

Then never again

My only crime was falling in love

Playing by the Rules

If friendship is the game, you want to play
Then play by the rules

I cannot stop myself from kissing you anymore then
you can stop yourself from wanting to kiss me
Even then I must play by rules

I cannot keep my hands away from yours anymore
then you can keep yours away from mine
Even then play I must play by the rules

I want to love you in every viable way since I cannot
get enough of you
Even then I must play by the rules

There is no room for such sweet games in friendship
I love you but I respect you even more

Unfortunately, neither one of us can admit to ourselves that we are both failing horribly at the game

Transitions

Before I met you
All I knew was how to survive

Now that I have met you
I want to live

Since you have to leave
I will transition back to simply existing

About the Author

Farzana Habib

Dripping

Farzana Habib is a 31 and a full time Scorpio who resides in Laval Quebec. She is a certified daycare educator and a student studying English and Education at Concordia University. She wants to work as a teacher and counselor after graduation. When she is away from her writing desk and computer, she can be found outside sightseeing, volunteering, or simply meeting new people and learning about diverse cultures.

www.ingramcontent.com/pod-product-compliance
Lightning Source LLC
LaVergne TN
LVHW041600070526
838199LV00046B/2065